DISNEY·PIXAR Cars 3 Taken by Storm

By **Bill Scollon** • Illustrated by the **Disney Storybook Art Team**

A Random House PICTUREBACK® Book

Random House 🏠 New York

Materials and characters from the movie *Cars 3*. Copyright © 2017 Disney Enterprises, Inc. and Pixar. All rights reserved.
Disney/Pixar elements © Disney/Pixar; rights in underlying vehicles are the property of the following third parties, as applicable: Hudson is a trademark of
FCA US LLC.; Chevrolet Impala is a trademark of General Motors; and Volkswagen trademarks, design patents and copyrights are used with the approval of the
owner, Volkswagen AG. Published in the United States by Random House Children's Books, a division of Penguin Random House LLC, 1745 Broadway,
New York, NY 10019, and in Canada by Penguin Random House Canada Limited, Toronto, in conjunction with Disney Enterprises, Inc. Pictureback,
Random House, and the Random House colophon are registered trademarks of Penguin Random House LLC.
randomhousekids.com
ISBN 978-0-7364-3727-1
Printed in the United States of America
10 9 8 7 6 5 4 3 2

THE RACING SEASON was in full swing, and Lightning McQueen was tearing up the track. But one day, a rookie named **Jackson Storm** came out of nowhere to take the checkered flag!

After the race, Lightning congratulated the new competitor.

"Hey—Jackson Storm, right? Great race today."

"Thank you, Mr. McQueen," said Storm. "You have no idea what a pleasure it is for me to finally beat you."

"Oh, thanks!" said Lightning. "Wait, hang on. Did you say **meet,** or **beat**?"

Storm gave Lightning a sideways glance. "I *think* you heard me."

Everyone was talking about Jackson Storm.
"Who is this **mysterious newcomer**?" Chick Hicks asked analyst Natalie Certain. "And why is he so darn fast?"

Natalie was an expert in racing efficiency. "Jackson Storm is part of the **Next Gens**. They're the next generation of high-tech racers," she said.

LOWER CENTER
OF GRAVITY

Jackson Storm continued to beat Lightning in race after race.

"Another easy win over old 'Ka-chow!'" Chick Hicks said during an interview with Storm. "Or should I say **'Ka-boose!'**— because he's always in the back! Am I right?"

"No, no, no, Chick. Lightning is a crafty veteran champ," said Storm. "He's the **elder statesman** of the sport, ya know?"

Racing fans cheered for the Next Gen as he headed for his transporter truck.

"Storm!" said one young fan. "Can I get an autograph?"

Jackson didn't stop, slow down, or even *look* at his fan. "Not now," he said. "I've got places to be."

Storm spent as much time as he could training on a racing simulator.

"That's six straight hours on the sim," Jackson's crew chief told him. "What do you say we mix it up?"

"Nah, I'm good," replied Storm.

"All right," his crew chief said. "Then let's go watch some film."

"For what? To see myself win *again*?" Storm asked.

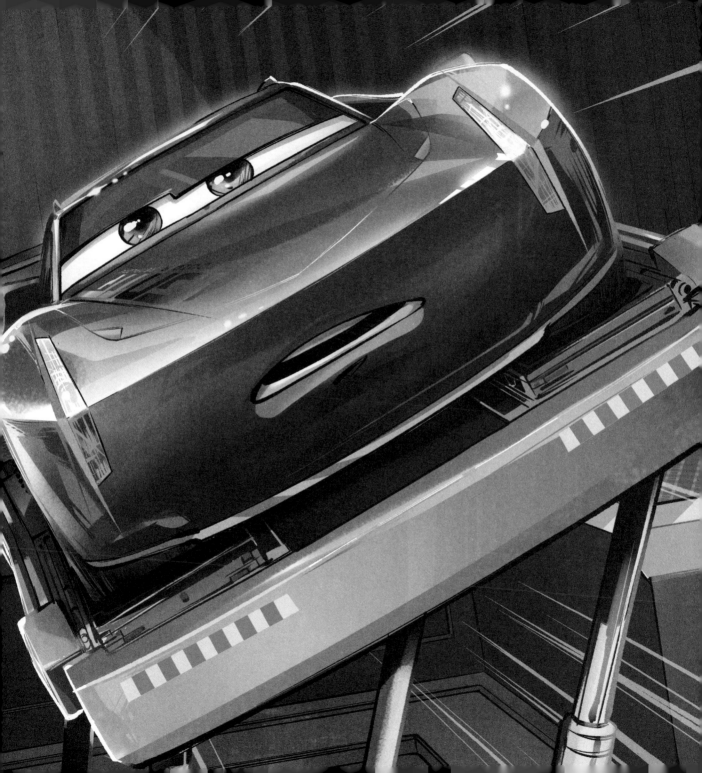

Meanwhile, Lightning McQueen traveled to Thomasville, Doc Hudson's hometown, to prepare for his rematch against Storm. He would train with Doc's old crew chief, **Smokey**.

Since Lightning needed a training partner, Smokey asked **Cruz Ramirez** to stand in as Storm. Cruz was an aspiring racer who was training Lightning.

To test Lightning's handling skills, Smokey released a herd of tractors. "Be *quick* or be *trampled*!" he yelled.

Later, at the local hangout, a **commercial** starring Storm
came on the big-screen TV. Storm smirked into the camera.
"My IGNTR Liquid Adrenaline will make you faster than
lightning!"

Lightning cringed. **"No way."**

Back at his racing headquarters, Storm was still busy training. The other Next Gens were in awe of him. They wanted to learn the **secrets to his success**.

"You're **amazing,** bro," said a fellow racer named Danny. "Can you give us some tips?"

"Don't interrupt a **champion** while he's training," replied Storm.

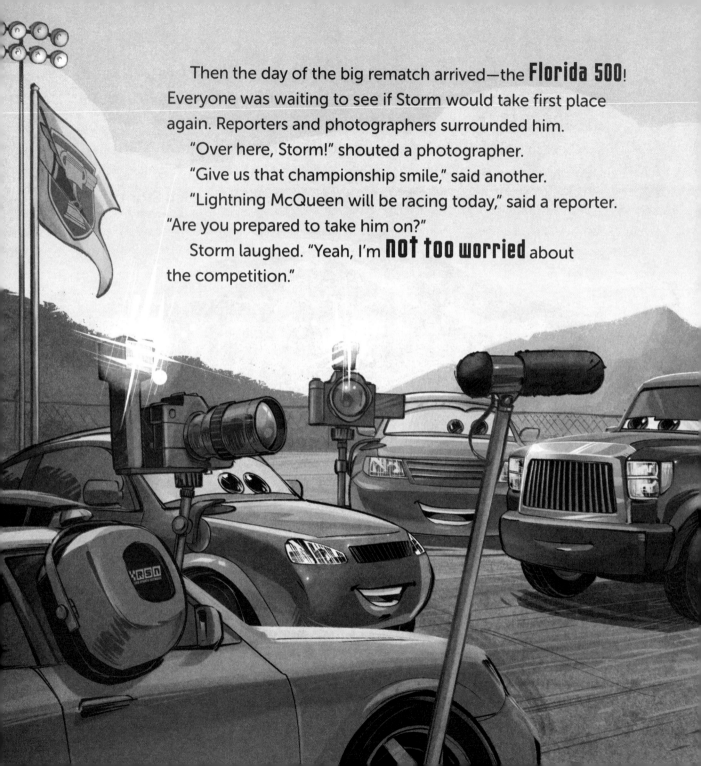

Then the day of the big rematch arrived—the **Florida 500**! Everyone was waiting to see if Storm would take first place again. Reporters and photographers surrounded him.

"Over here, Storm!" shouted a photographer.

"Give us that championship smile," said another.

"Lightning McQueen will be racing today," said a reporter. "Are you prepared to take him on?"

Storm laughed. "Yeah, I'm **not too worried** about the competition."

Chick Hicks cornered Storm for an interview. "How are you feeling, champ?"

"Better than ever," said Storm. "I'm here to *win,* and that's what I'm going to do."

A reporter called to the Next Gen, "Can I get a picture?"

"Sure thing," replied Storm. "Sorry, Chick. I gotta cut this short."

"Let's get you and one of your fans together," said the reporter.

Storm drove up to the young fan who had tried to get his attention before. "It's your lucky day," he told him. "You must be *excited* to finally meet me."

"Not anymore," said the fan. "And I don't want to be in your picture."

"Your loss," said Storm. "I gotta get to the track anyway."

Just then, Lightning McQueen drove by.

"Enjoy your *last race*," said Storm. "Hope you can make it past lap twenty."

Lightning paid no attention to Storm as he zoomed onto the track.

All the racers started scrubbing their tires and doing laps, waiting for the green flag to drop.

When the race began, Lightning skillfully made his way through the pack, gaining on Storm.

Suddenly, some of the racers **crashed** into each other. The yellow flag came out, signaling to all the cars to move off the track.

Lightning pulled into the pit and turned to his team. "Get *Cruz* out there. I want her to finish the race."

Without a second to lose, the Radiator Springs gang went to work.

In the press box, Chick Hicks was shocked. "I've **never** seen this before!"

"Unbelievable," said Natalie Certain. "For once, I have **no** predictions for how this is going to turn out."

At first, Cruz felt *nervous*. Lightning, now acting as her crew chief, reminded her of their training in Thomasville. Cruz started to **race her heart out**.

Eventually, she caught up to Storm. He saw that she was nearing the wall, so he *slammed* **her** right into it!

Cruz gathered her wits. She knew exactly what she needed to do. She forced her tires up onto the wall—and *flipped* over Storm! When Cruz came back down to the track, she was in **FIRST** place!

Storm crossed the finish line **behind** Cruz.
The crowd went crazy!

Storm looked on as Cruz and Lightning celebrated. He couldn't believe he'd been beaten by a **ROOKIE**.

In Victory Lane, Cruz was surrounded by the press.

"You came out of nowhere to beat Storm," said a reporter. "How'd you do it?"

"I learned from the *best*," said Cruz, smiling at her friend Lightning.

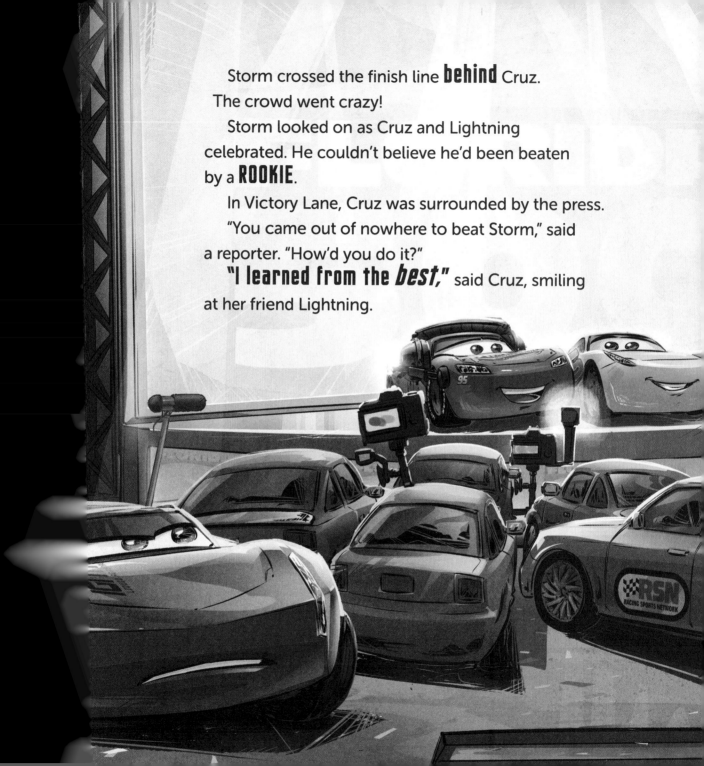

So what are you waiting for?
Let your engine ROAR!

Now you're living your dream! And once you get started, who knows how far you can go? You might even surprise **yourself**!

Be sure to listen to your **CREW CHIEF**.
He'll remind you to **believe** in **YOURSELF**.

When **your moment** comes and it's time to enter the race, don't doubt yourself. **SEIZE THE OPPORTUNITY!**

Soon all that practice will pay off. There's nothing like the feeling of roaring into the homestretch knowing you're **better** than you were yesterday!

Put your **heart and soul** into working hard. Give it everything you've got!

Want to know how to **outthink** and **outrace** every other car on the track? Take a spin with the Legends and *listen* to their stories.

And sometimes things will get **messy**.

Other great racers have defeated the odds, and **YOU** can, too! Pick yourself up, wash yourself off, and get ready for your next race!

Sometimes things will get
OUT OF CONTROL.

Don't always train in the same old places with the same old faces. That's the quickest way to get stuck in a rut. Go **outside** your comfort zone. Make new friends!

At first you might feel **uneasy** about trying
something new. But don't give up! Before you know
it, you'll be blasting down the beach!

You just need to find **YOUR** thing. To do that, you have to keep trying **new tactics**. Nervous about losing traction on the sand? Scared of spinning out? **USE THAT!**

But remember that **everyone is different**. Training that might make one car better might not work for you. **That's all right!**

Even the best racers—like Lightning
McQueen—need **practice** to improve.
So get ready to train and work hard!

Then race toward your goal!

Everyone starts **somewhere**. Me? I started as a trainer. I helped other cars train on the racing simulator to become faster and smarter racers.

Before your tires hit the track, there's one thing to remember: you have to **LOVE** racing! Wake up feeling the need for speed. Fall asleep thinking of the wind whipping past you on the speedway. And dream of crossing the finish line first!

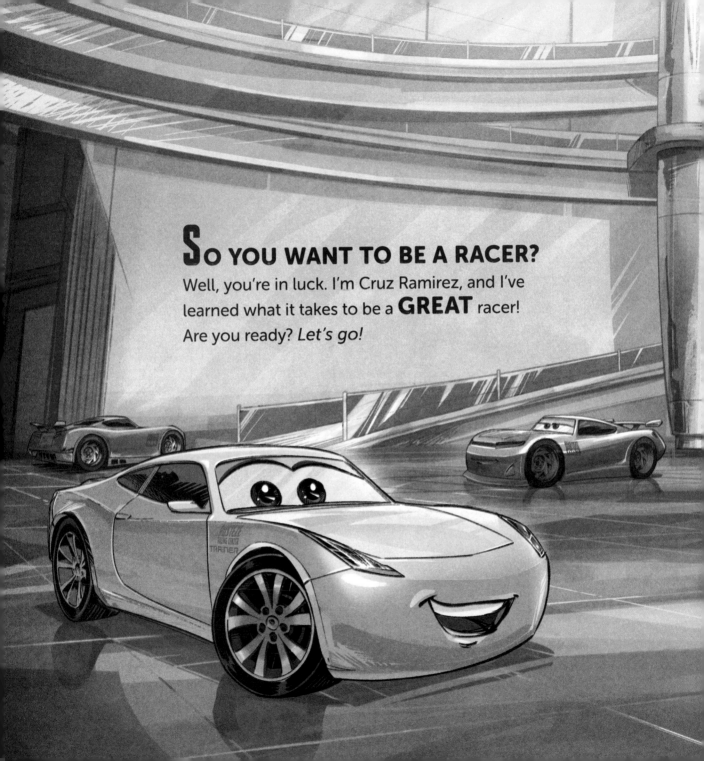

So you want to be a racer?

Well, you're in luck. I'm Cruz Ramirez, and I've learned what it takes to be a **GREAT** racer! Are you ready? *Let's go!*

Disney · PIXAR

Cars 3

How to Be a Great Racer

By **Liz Marsham**

Illustrated by the **Disney Storybook Art Team**

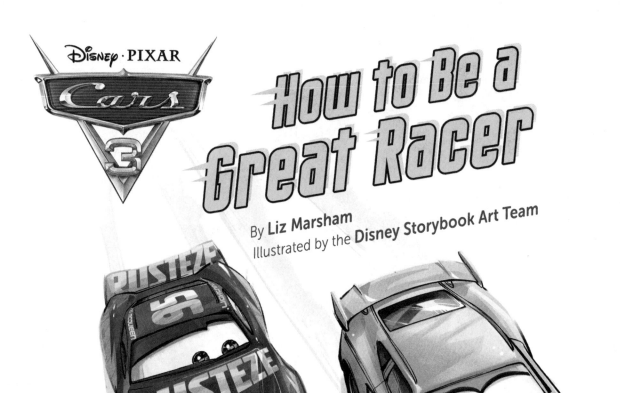

A Random House PICTUREBACK® Book

Random House 🏠 New York

Materials and characters from the movie *Cars 3*. Copyright © 2017 Disney Enterprises, Inc. and Pixar. All rights reserved.
Disney/Pixar elements © Disney/Pixar; rights in underlying vehicles are the property of the following third parties, as applicable: Hudson, Hudson Hornet, and Nash Ambassador are trademarks of FCA US LLC.; Chevrolet Impala is a trademark of General Motors; FIAT is a trademark of FCA Group Marketing S.p.A.; and Volkswagen trademarks, design patents and copyrights are used with the approval of the owner, Volkswagen AG. Published in the United States by Random House Children's Books, a division of Penguin Random House LLC, 1745 Broadway, New York, NY 10019, and in Canada by Penguin Random House Canada Limited, Toronto, in conjunction with Disney Enterprises, Inc. Pictureback, Random House, and the Random House colophon are registered trademarks of Penguin Random House LLC.
randomhousekids.com
ISBN 978-0-7364-3727-1
Printed in the United States of America
10 9 8 7 6 5 4 3 2